A MESSAGE TO PARENTS

Reading good books to young children is a crucial factor in a child's psychological and intellectual development. It promotes a mutually warm and satisfying relationship between parent and child and enhances the child's awareness of the world around him. It stimulates the child's imagination and lays a foundation for the development of the skills necessary to support the critical thinking process. In addition, the parent who reads to his child helps him to build vocabulary and other prerequisite skills for the child's own successful reading.

In order to provide parents and children with books which will do these things, Brown Watson has published this series of small books specially designed for young children. These books are factual, fanciful, humorous, questioning and adventurous. A library acquired in this inexpensive way will provide many hours of pleasurable and profitable reading for parents and children.

Published by Brown Watson (Leicester) Ltd.
ENGLAND
© 1980 Rand McNally & Company
Printed and bound in the German Democratic Republic.

Little Toy Train

By Catherine Stahlmann
Illustrated by Dean Bryant

Brown Watson

England.

LITTLE Toy Train was a goods train. He had a shiny engine, three wagons, a coal van, and a bright red guard's van. Whenever he sped around his track in one corner of the playroom he called out gaily, "Chug-chug! Chug-chug!" His bell tinkled merrily as he raced over the familiar route.

First, there was the tiny village with its station and shops, its houses and trees and church.

Then, there was the high hill that he chugged up ever so slowly, but whizzed down, lickety-split!

Next was the long, dark mountain tunnel and the bridge which spanned the glassy blue lake. And he was back at the village station.

One day, after many trips around the track, Little Toy Train said sadly,

"It's always the same. Every time I chug up the hill, I whizz down it. Every time I whizz down the hill,

I go through the tunnel. Every time I come out of the tunnel, I cross the bridge. Then I'm here again at the station! I wish I could do something different, just once!"

His wish did not come true –

at least not then. One night, how-
ever, when everything was quiet,
Little Toy Train discovered that
someone had taken him off his
track and had forgotten to put
him back. Moonlight glistened

through the windows, so he could
see his village, but he did not know
how to get there. He tried to
move.

"Chug-chug! Chug-chug!" he
said slowly.

Then he said it faster – "Chug-chug! Chug-chug!"

Little Toy Train began to move. His silvery wheels went round and round. His headlight blinked on and off like a firefly. His bell tinkled merrily.

"I can move without my track!"

he said happily. "Now I can do something different!"

"Chug-chug! Chug-chug!" he said as he went under the wheels of a tricycle.

Suddenly his light went off, and he bumped into something soft.

"Ouch!" someone cried. "Do look where you are going, Little Toy Train!"

Little Toy Train's headlight blinked on again. He saw that he had bumped into Teddy Bear.

"I'm so sorry," he said. "My light doesn't work well when I'm off my track doing something different. Please excuse me."

"That's all right," said Teddy Bear. "You didn't really hurt me. Have fun, Little Toy Train."

Little Toy Train chugged along in front of Teddy Bear and the other toys sitting beside him – Baby Doll, Rocking Horse, Furry Kitten, Cowboy, and Cuddly Dog. They all smiled at him.

"You seem to be having lots of fun, Little Toy Train," said Cowboy.

"Indeed I am!" he answered. "I'm doing something different!"

"How about giving me a ride?"

asked Cowboy. "I'll sit on top of your guard's van and pretend I'm riding a horse."

"All right," said Little Toy Train.

With Cowboy on his guard's van, Little Toy Train raced across the floor. Suddenly there was a big round object straight in front of him – a red rubber ball. He knew he

would never be able to stop in time to avoid an accident. But when he crashed into the ball, a very funny thing happened. The ball just rolled away. It was so funny that Little Toy Train did it again and again.

"This is more fun than horse-riding!" exclaimed Cowboy.

When Little Toy Train rammed into the ball again, Cowboy laughed so much he fell off the van. He decided that he had had enough riding, so Little Toy Train went on alone.

He chugged past some toy sol-
diers and a drum, past a doll's house
and an aeroplane. He was enjoying
himself so much that he did not
realise his headlight was out again.

He did not realise it until he discovered he could see nothing at all. Even the moonlight was gone. He had zoomed into a toy tent.

"I'm lost!" he said. He went round and round trying to find a

way out, but without a light, it was impossible to see anything.

"Help! Help!" he called.

Something rubbed against him. It frightened him.

"Help! Help!" he called again.

"Don't be scared, Little Toy Train. I'm Furry Kitten. With my green eyes I can see in the dark. I'll help you. Let me hook my tail into your bumper, and I'll pull you out!"

And sure enough, Furry Kitten
did just that. He pulled Little Toy
Train back to the very spot where
his night's adventure had started.

Later that day, after someone had put him back on his track, Little Toy Train again chugged up and down the hill, through the tunnel, across the bridge, and through the village to the station.